BOWWOW: BOOK OF
WINSTON'S
WORDS OF WISDOM

LINDA APPLE

Illustrations by DYLAN HALE

LEE
PRESS

an imprint of
YOUNG DRAGONS PRESS

OGHMA

CREATIVE MEDIA

Bentonville, Arkansas • Los Angeles, California
www.oghmacreative.com

Library of Congress Cataloging-in-Publication Data

Names: Apple, Linda C, author.
Title: Book of Winston's Words of Wisdom/Linda C. Apple
Description: First Edition. | Bentonville: Lee, 2020.
Identifiers: LCCN: 2020944345 | ISBN: 978-1-63373-631-3 (hardcover) |
ISBN: 978-1-63373-632-0 (trade paperback) | ISBN: 978-1-63373-633-7 (eBook)
Subjects: | BISAC: JUVENILE FICTION/Animals/Dogs |
JUVENILE FICTION/Readers/Chapter Books |
JUVENILE FICTION/Social Themes/Values & Virtues
LC record available at: https://lccn.loc.gov/2020944345

Lee Press paperback edition September, 2020

Illustration and Design by Dylan Hale
Interior Design by Casey W. Cowan
Editing by Chrissy Willis, Derek Hale, Patty Stith, & Amy Cowan

Published by Lee Press, an imprint of Young Dragons Press, a subsidiary of The Oghma Book Group. Find out more at www.youngdragonspress.com.

I dedicate this book to my grandchildren,
to my great-grandchildren yet to be born,
and to all generations after them.
I may not get to meet you on this earth,
but I want you to know you were in my heart.

You all are special. You all have purpose.
Love, Nonni

TABLE OF CONTENTS

❖ ACKNOWLEDGMENTS

High Paw!

Loving gratitude for my biggest fans, my husband, Neal, my children: Amanda, Rob, Charles, Olivia, and William. Thank you to Casey Cowan, Chrissy Willis, Dylan Hale, and the staff of Oghma Creative Media. Special thanks to Karsyn Apple. Her edits to Winston's stories were so helpful and spot on!

✿ CHANGE

Change can be hard, but it can be good, too.

High paw everyone! Winston Apple here, the TDIC (Top Dog in Charge) of Apple security, with my latest report: Change.

It has been a slow day here as far as my security watch goes. Boring, actually. It is a cold, gray day, and it is raining. Squirrels don't like rain, so they are curled up in their nests in the trees. The deer are bedded down somewhere on the hillside. So here I am with nothing to do but snuggle on my bed and snooze. But I can't sleep because thoughts keep dancing in my head. In other words, I'm remembering how I came to be the TDIC of Apple Security.

I was born in Texas and was one of four litter mates. We lived in what our lady-human called a kennel. Our momma took good care of us. I liked the way her soft tongue felt on my face when she washed me. In my mind I can still taste the warm, sweet milk she fed us and feel her soft tummy where I fell asleep when my belly was full.

When I woke from my nap, my brother and sisters and I wrestled and played tug of war with an old sock. Our kennel was surrounded with a fence, and on pretty days we played chase outside.

One morning our lady-human came to our kennel and gave us a dish of something soft and delicious. We actually had to use our teeth to chew it. Our mom said we had grown enough to eat solid food and that we no longer needed her milk. That made me kinda sad, but I always looked forward to our lady-human bringing that dish of yummy. Yep. Life was good, and I liked it just the way it was. I never wanted it to change.

But it did.

The change started when a man and a little

girl came to our kennel and played with us. It was nice, that is, until the little girl said, "Daddy, I want this one."

She held up my sister, and before I knew it, they got into something Mom called a car and off they went. A few days later, a man and woman took my other sister. They got in their car and drove away. What was going on? I did not like this. Not one little bit. But when I yipped my complaint to my mom, she touched my nose with hers and said this was just a part of growing up.

Then came the day when a man came to our kennel. He squatted down and spoke with a kind voice to me and my brother. Then he picked me up and told our lady-human he wanted me. He took me to his car and put me in a metal cage with a soft pillow and closed the door. BowWowsers! What a strange feeling. The ground beneath me rumbled and swayed. Houses and trees blurred by. I don't mind telling you, that was scary, so I buried my face in my paws and stopped watching.

After what seemed like forever, the man took me into a strange house and held me out to another lady-human. "Surprise, Sugar!"

The lady took me in her arms and said, "Babe, I love him."

Even as a pup, I was quick to catch on. My new humans didn't have to tell me their names. I figured it out by myself that the lady's name was Sugar, and the man's was Babe. Sugar cuddled me up to her chest and said, "You look like a Winston, so that is your new name."

I liked my new name. I liked Sugar and Babe. But even though it felt nice being cuddled to Sugar's chest, I still felt confused and lonely. A little bit later, Sugar put something called a collar around my neck, showed me my new bed and a bunch of new toys. I gave all of those things a sniff, still unsure and frightened. Then she gave me a bowl of food. Finally, something familiar! I buried my nose in the dish and gobbled it up.

When I finished, she clasped a long rope to my collar, took me outside, and told me to go potty.

Potty?

What the woof was that?

And how did she expect me to do anything with that rope on my neck? I just sat down not knowing what she wanted. Worry and sadness

filled me. I wanted to go back to my kennel. I wanted my mom. I wanted my brother and sisters. I wanted to run free. But here I was being told to "potty."

All I knew is that I needed to go pee-pee, and I couldn't hold it any longer, so I did. You should have seen Sugar. She whooped and patted me and gave me a treat. Arf! I'd pee-pee every hour for a treat. The weird thing was, when I went potty inside, well, you don't even want to know what happened then. I don't mind telling you, I was one confused puppy.

As time went by, I learned that it was okay to piddle outside but not inside. I liked my bed, my toys, and Sugar and Babe became my folks. I loved snuggling on Sugar's soft lap and the soothing feel of her petting my back and scratching behind my ears. I had rip-roaring times playing catch, chase, and tug of war with Babe. And the new house? It was now my house. And as I grew, I knew my place in it.

I was The Top Dog In Charge.

When a destructive deer came close to my folks' flowers, I sounded the alarm. When a sneaky squirrel tried to raid their bird feeders, I barked a warning. If someone walked on our porch and knocked on our door, I woofed an announcement and made sure to let whoever was on the other side know that I was watching them, so no funny stuff. Well, that was until they scratched behind my ears. Then I knew they were okay, and I could go play.

So much had changed from my life at the kennel. But as time went by all that was new and strange became familiar and comfortable. I loved my folks, and they loved me. I had my own bed, toys, food, and yummy treats. I also had a new friend, the folks' grandson, Soren.

Yeppers, life is good. I sure hope my brother and sisters are as happy as me. Arf!

Change happens in sooo many ways. For me, my family changed. I moved from one home where I knew everyone and felt comfortable and happy to a new house in a different town where everything was different, and everyone was a stranger. I changed too. I grew up and had to learn new things.

Change can be hard. Some people like it, and some don't. At first, I didn't. With a little time, though, I found my place in my new surroundings. I learned my new responsibilities, and I watched my ever-changing body grow.

Change reminds me of the plants in Sugar's garden. I've watched her plant a bean seed in dirt, and you know what? When that seed came out of the ground, it didn't look the same. It had changed into a little green sprout. And it kept changing. It grew tall, and big leaves sprouted from its stem. Then flowers bloomed on it, and those blooms turned into beans. Why am I telling you this? Because I've seen that everything living grows and changes. Change. It's just what living things do.

WINSTON WONDERS?

What kind of changes have you experienced? How did they make you feel? Even though things have changed, what are some things that remained the same?

THINGS ARE NOT ALWAYS AS THEY SEEM

Even we smart dogs can be fooled.

High paw everyone! Winston Apple here, the TDIC (Top Dog in Charge) of Apple security, with my latest report: Moving Rocks.

The day started out as the perfect fall day. My buddy, Soren, came over to play. Remember him? He is the folks' grandson. He's eight years old. I really love that guy. He has the kindest blue eyes, and when he smiles it is like the sun rising. Just brightens up my day. As soon as his folks dropped him off, he slapped his hands on his knees and said, "Come on, Winston." We ran outside to explore the woods. In the crisp breeze we chased the red and yellow leaves twirling down from the trees. After a while, Soren went to the creek bed to hunt for fossils, and I hunted for sneaky squirrels and damaging deer. That is when it happened. When I discovered something really strange.

Are you ready for this?

I saw a moving rock. Yeppers, you read that right. A rock that stood on four feet and walked. No kidding! I'm not pulling your tail!

I happened to be sniffing a tree where another dog had left a pee mail. That's sort of like your email, only since we dogs can't type with our paws, we lift our legs and leave our messages that way.

So back to the moving rock. It all started when I heard a rustling sound. I scanned the area to make sure it wasn't a sneaky squirrel, and that's when I noticed a rock moving away from me. I blinked, not believing my eyes. But there it was, walking! Peoples, this called for a closer look. I followed the rock as close as I dared and then, when I got near enough to give it a good sniffing, its legs disappeared.

Gone! Just like that. Poof!

The thing just laid there looking like any other rock. I wasn't fooled, though. My security instincts took over. As the TDIC it was my job to check this thing out. I had to be sly in order to keep from frightening Soren. So I snuck up beside it to get a good look.

First, I made a visual examination. The rock had what looked like circles down its middle with squares on either side of the circles. The rock was brown, but the circles and squares were outlined in yellow. A shiver tingled down my spine. Could this rock actually be an alien? Something from another planet? Were these symbols? A secret message? Were we being invaded? A growl almost escaped into my throat, but I swallowed it down. No need to worry my buddy Soren just yet.

Second, I conducted a full-nose modus operandi, meaning I gave that rock a good sniffing. It had a musty, damp smell. Like pond water. Reminded me a little of a snake.

SNAKE? YIKES!

Have you ever seen a squatty-legged Scottish

Terrier jump five feet in the air? Well, you didn't, and I'm not admitting to anything.

Finally, I took the wait-and-see approach. I stepped back, not because it smelled like a—ahem—snake or anything. No, not at all. And then, while watching it, something even stranger happened. The rock's bottom half parted open from its top half and two beady, orange eyes stared at me. Yes! The rock had eyes!

Well, that was enough for me. I gave it a full-on barking. Then I ran to Soren and howled, "Aliens! Danger! Let's get out of here! We gotta go tell the folks."

Soren stopped what he was doing and ran over to see what made me sound the alarm. I danced all around that alien rock, doing my most impressive moves jumping back and forth while uttering vicious growls.

When Soren saw the rock, you know what he did? He picked it up. That was one of the bravest things I'd ever seen him do. When he touched it, the weird little thing shut tight, which annoyed me because he would never believe the rock had eyes. I waited for him to sound the alarm, run to the house and tell the folks we were being invaded. But he didn't. Instead, he laughed.

Huh? My jaw dropped. I couldn't believe my ears. We were about to be invaded by alien rocks, and he was laughing? Well, I always knew that by dog standards he wasn't the brightest chew-toy on the shelf, but this was serious!

He put the rock down and said, "What's wrong Winston. Is this turtle scaring you?"

Turtle?

Ok, on a closer look, the rock did appear to be a turtle. Hey, in my defense it really looked like a rock, and if the rock had moved on legs and had beady, orange eyes, it could have been an alien. Right?

The worst part of this whole ordeal was that while doing my duty as the TDIC, Soren was laughing at me. Grrrr. Just wait and see if I ever protect him again… never again. I might just quit my job and find someone else to protect. Somewhere I'm appreciated.

When we returned home, he reported to Sugar and Babe about my little mistake. Did they tell Soren he should have been ashamed for laughing at the TDIC while doing his job? No. You know what they did? They laughed too. Needless to say, I was humiliated. I went to my pillow, circled it, and flopped down with a heavy sigh. Truth be known, even though thoughts of quitting were tempting, I knew I'd never quit my job. Apple security is in my blood. So, let them laugh. I'll just wait for the day when an alien rock *does* come to earth. Then we will see who has the last bark. Arf!

Sometimes things look one way but are really something else. For instance, some little dogs seem unfriendly to me because they yap and snap, but I think it is because they are afraid of larger dogs and want to appear brave.

Maybe your human seems angry with you, but on the other paw maybe your human is just tired. I once heard Soren say he thought a kid at school didn't like him, only to find out that the kid was just really shy.

There are always two sides to a situation. So take the wait-and-see approach. Who knows, with time you might realize that the moving rock you see is really a turtle!

WINSTON WONDERS?

Have you been fooled by something that wasn't what it seemed? Have you ever thought someone wasn't your friend, but when you started playing with them, you had a lot in common? Have you ever misunderstood something a friend said to you and got your feelers hurt? Things like this sometimes happen. Sometimes you just need to have a yap about it and straighten things out.

A NEW LEASH ON LIFE

Leashes—The Good, The Bad, and The Necessary

High paw everyone! Winston Apple here, the TDIC (Top Dog in Charge) of Apple security, with my latest report: Lousy Leashes.

The other day I made a bad choice. A really, really, bad choice. I could have been hurt really bad... or even worse, my best buddy, Soren, could have been hurt, too.

Before I report on what happened, I will start by explaining why I made that bad choice. When my folks, Babe and Sugar, sold our house in the country, we moved from a large house in the middle of the woods to a small rental house in town that had a teeny, tiny backyard.

It was on a busy street—more like a racetrack. I went from being a country dog to a city dog. In the country I could run and run and run. The loudest noises I ever heard were birds.

In the city I couldn't run anywhere and had to listen to cars' varooming engines, sirens, and booming bass music. It was so loud, the window where I kept watch vibrated! BowWowsers!

How I missed spending the days keeping destructive deer from the folks' garden and chasing sneaky squirrels up trees where they belonged. At our new place there were no deer, but there were plenty of squirrels. Unlike country squirrels, these city rodents had no respect for their superiors.

They actually robbed my folks' bird feeders and ate the seeds. One even sat and stared at me while I glared at him through the window! I woof you not! But could I do anything about it? In a word— no. Why, you ask? Because this country dog now lived in the city, and because of that, I had to wear a doggone leash.

Leashes. I hate them. I wanted to roam and play anywhere I chose, like I used to. But no, the folks insisted that while in town, I had to stay on a leash. If I could have talked I would have asked them, "Then how do you expect me to do my job as TDIC with a leash attached to my neck?" BowWowsers, impossible! Even worse? I was the laughingstock of squirrels because they knew I couldn't chase them. Grrrr.

However, living in town did have a few—very few—positive things. Even though I had to wear that doggone leash, there were nice walking trails in the city with some very interesting pee mail around the trees and bushes that grew on either side of the paved paths.

Confused? Lemme explain. You know how adults read email on their computers and phones? Remember, we dogs leave pee mail and we read this mail with our noses. That's right! With our noses.

So, the entire way I read the trees and bushes and left a few messages of my own. Well… actually a lot of messages. The frustrating part about those trails were the people on bikes.

It never failed that while reading a particularly interesting pee mail on the opposite side of the trail someone always cycled toward us or warned us with their bell that they were about to pass us, and Sugar had to yank me away with that crummy leash. She didn't care the least little bit that I'd just come to the best part of the message.

Grrrr.

Now on to my bad choice. The day started out as perfect as a dog in the city could want. My buddy, Soren, came over to play. After we ran around the house and wrestled a bit, Soren asked Sugar, "May Winston and I go outside for a while?"

To my surprise, she said yes and even let me go with him leash free! Ahhh, the freedom felt wonderful. We flopped down in the soft grass and rolled on our backs to stare at the puffy clouds drifting across the blue sky.

Soren liked to imagine what animals the clouds looked like. I just liked being next to him. While we lazed in the warm sunshine, I saw something move in the tree above us. That squirrel! And this time there was no window blocking me from him. Ha! I'd teach him!

Immediately, I went into TDIC mode. Apple security was in danger. The birdseed was in danger. I jumped up on all four legs and zeroed in on that pest. A low rumble sounded in my throat warning that rat with a fancy tail that there was no glass between us now. He ran down the tree, anyway.

Well, peoples, that did it. In my TDIC doggy brain, all systems were go. I charged toward him baring my teeth which should have scared him to death. But you know what he did? The silly thing raced across that busy street… and I kinda, sorta, well… I ran across that busy street, too.

Drivers in the cars slammed on their brakes, screeching to a stop. I didn't notice, though. I was zeroed in on that bushy tail. Then, just as I was closing in on that rascal, I heard Soren scream, "Winston! No!"

I turned around to see him starting to cross the road after me, and BowWowsers, he didn't look for cars, either. To heck with the squirrel, I had to save Soren. I sprinted back across the road toward him, not looking this time either because I had to act fast. Once again, there was the noise of slamming brakes and screeching tires.

By now Sugar was outside with Soren. I saw that look of Terrier on their faces, and my tail automatically curled between my legs and underneath my belly. My alert ears fell down. I did my best to look sorry for what I had done.

Peoples, I knew I was in big trouble. Sugar gave us a good yapping. She put me back on the leash, but I didn't howl because I knew I'd made a bad choice. A *really* bad choice.

When Sugar went back in the house, Soren and I stayed outside. He sat next to me and rubbed my back. I licked away the tears on his face. While we shared this quiet moment together, I thought about what had just happened. I watched the cars flash by on the street I had just dashed across. You know? I could have been one flat dog.

Even worse, Soren might have followed me and been flattened, too. I put my head on my paws and sighed. Maybe a leash wasn't such a bad thing. After all, I never knew when my brain would go all wonky and change into *get that squirrel mode*. At least a leash will keep me from hurting myself, and even more important, keep my best buddy safe, too.

As a wise dog once said, "In everything there is a reason, a time to leash and a time to unleash, a time to chase squirrels and a time to just let those rascals cross the road by themselves."

You could say that leashes are like boundaries and are there for our protection. You may not wear a leash, but you may be told what you can and cannot do, which feels like a leash to you. You may want to ride your bike in the street, but your human tells you no. You may want to play in the park with your friends after dark, but your human calls you home. Your people may not let you stay up late on a school night or eat all the sweets you want. Take it from me, though, it is because they care.

When I ignored the boundaries the folks gave me and went into squirrel-chasing mode, I not only put my life in danger, but my best friend's too. As much as I hated that yucky leash, it was there for my protection. And, it is the same way with you. Your peoples want you to be healthy and safe. Remember that, okay? Arf!

WINSTON WONDERS?

What are some things you want to do, but those who care for you say you can't because it isn't safe? Why do you think people say no to you when it is something you really want to do? What are some better choices you can make?

☙ TRAPPED!

There is a Time to Bark.

High paw everyone! Winston Apple here, the TDIC (Top Dog in Charge) of Apple security, with my latest report: Trapped.

We all are different, right? Some of us are shy, not knowing what to say or do. Some of us are bold, knowing exactly what to say and do. Some of us dogs bark like crazy, no matter what the reason—it could be something as simple as a beetle bug crawling on the porch. And some of us just don't bark at all.

I'm one of those that don't bark. There are a

few exceptions, however, when I do. Like when someone holds up my favorite toy, a stuffed hedgehog, and wants to play. Then, you better believe I'll bark. Or when there is a disturbance in the Force by a sneaky squirrel or a destructive deer, I'll sound the alarm.

If somebody is knocking on the front door of our new house, I'll alert the family. Other than that, I'm pretty chill. This has worked out pretty good for me—until the other day when I was trapped! Yep, you read me right. Trapped with no way out.

Here's what happened. My buddy, Soren, came to the folks' house to play. All morning long we ran through the grass scaring grasshoppers and making them fly away with a clicking sound. Then we explored the woods checking the creek for tadpoles. Finally, we went back to the yard and played a game of fetch the stick. We had a woofin' good time.

I don't mind telling you, I was one bushed dog by the end of the morning and hungry as a bear. Soren was, too, so we trotted to the house for a snack. Soren had a yummy cheese stick that he shared with me. But that was all we could have before lunch. So, while we waited, Soren and I relaxed and watched a little television.

He sprawled out on the recliner, and I circled the small area under the recliner and plopped down. It didn't take long for me to get bored with all the *blah, blah, blah* on the television, and soon I was sound asleep.

I was having the greatest dream. One of my favorites, actually. It's the one where I am chasing a squirrel, and when it scampers up the tree, I do too. I run straight up the trunk with my bare paws like I'm running on the ground. Ever have that dream? Dawg, it's great! Okay, back to my dream. So I follow the squirrel and leap from branch to branch in close pursuit. Just as I was about to sink my teeth in its bushy tail, though, I heard a thunk! My eyes flew open, and I jumped, only, I couldn't stand up.

Why, you may wonder?

Well, Soren was called to lunch, and he totally forgot about me. Can you believe that? Forgetting the TDIC? Not only did he forget me, he left me trapped under the recliner. *Under* it! While he was enjoying the meat treat goodies with the folks, I was left all alone in that dark, cramped space.

To make things worse, the delicious aromas of lunch kept wafting past my super-sensitive nose. My stomach rumbled. I should have been with them so I could clean up after them. You see, sometimes they drop food on the floor, and I lick it up right away. Floor duty is one of my favorite responsibilities as the TDIC. Well, a messy floor served them right for leaving me trapped under the chair.

Surely, I thought, I would soon be missed and rescued. I crouched under there for what seemed like forever. Peoples, I seriously considered barking, but I finally heard my name being called. I relaxed knowing it wouldn't be long until they found me. At first, they called in their most sweet voices. I whimpered back, forgetting they didn't have the same excellent ears as me. I guess they didn't hear me.

I decided to go ahead and bark, that is, until I heard their voices had changed to an angry sound. The folks yelled, "Winston, you come

here right this minute." Uh-oh. When they call me like that, it usually meant I'm in big trouble. Maybe being trapped and out of sight wasn't such a bad thing, after all.

I listened to them call me as they went into every room in the house and then outside. They sounded frustrated and kept fussing about how I knew better than to run off. They had decided I was out chasing a deer. And they were angry about that? Wasn't that my job?

While I cowered under the chair, I worried. What if they come back to this room? Should I bark? If I did, would I be in trouble? I decided to keep silent.

Finally, Soren said, "He can't be outside. None of us opened the door. Where was I the last time I saw him?" Then he snapped his fingers. "I remember! He was under the recliner." He paused, then said, "Uh-oh."

Fast footsteps approached where I was trapped. Soren pulled up the footrest and peeked under the recliner. "Winston? Are you okay?"

I still wasn't sure if I should bark, so instead I gave a tiny shake of my collar, causing my tags to jingle. He yelled, "I found him." Then he helped me out from underneath the chair, picked me up, and snuggled me, saying, "You poor boy. I'm so sorry."

Hearing the love in his voice, I barked, "I'm fine. No harm done." Just to show my forgiveness I gave a big, sloppy lick on the cheek.

It felt good to be free. Everyone loved on me, giving me pats and scratches behind my ears. Even better, they gave me meat treats. After a while, everyone decided to watch television. This time, instead of getting under the recliner, I jumped up on the footrest, snuggled down, and napped there. Hey, I'm not making that mistake again. Now if only I could go back to my favorite dream. Arf!

Sometimes when we have a problem, we may not speak up because we think we might get in trouble or that we made a bad mistake. We might be embarrassed. So, we just keep our mouths shut. But that doesn't help us. Remember how I was trapped under the chair? I didn't bark, so I stayed trapped.

If you ever feel trapped, speak up. If someone hurts you or threatens to hurt you or someone you love, speak up. If you are confused and need help in school, don't worry about what others think, speak up. Never be ashamed of asking for help, because we all learn differently.

Bark up, everyone. How about it? Deal?

WINSTON WONDERS?

Have you ever made a big mistake and thought you might get in trouble? Has someone ever frightened or bullied you? Has something or someone made you feel uncomfortable? Listen to Winston—speak up!

WHO SAYS DOGS CAN'T LIKE CATS?

Just Because We Are Different Doesn't Mean We Cannot Be Friends

High paw everyone! Winston Apple here, the TDIC (Top Dog in Charge) of Apple security, with my latest report: Cats. Yes, cats.

When I first moved in with my folks, Sugar and Babe, I soon learned I wasn't the only pet at the house. They also had two outdoor cats, Gypsy and Dickens.

Right away I knew I liked Gypsy. She was black like me, and we were about the same size. Gypsy liked me, too. In fact, she took care of me as if I were her very own kitten. She snuggled me when I napped on the porch, and she groomed me when I needed it.

On the other paw, I was kinda afraid of Dickens. He was huge, and his fur was so gray it looked purple. He kept his distance, and I kept mine. But as time went by, we became friends, and we played. My only bark with playing chase with him was that he could climb the trees with his sharp fingers. Then he'd sit on a branch and laugh at me. That was okay, though. We were just having fun.

I had always had cat friends. So imagine my surprise when a neighbor dog told me that dogs were not supposed to like cats. He woofed how dogs were smarter, and cats were goofy. He called them sneaky and said they were not to be trusted. Warning me that if I was caught playing with a cat, other dogs wouldn't be my friend.

That dog's view about cats left a squirmy feeling inside me. Like a worm tying itself into a knot. I didn't like it. Were cats sneaky? Were they really not very smart?

Later that afternoon, I watched Dickens hunt a mole. He sat really still and waited and waited and waited until just the right time and then *bam!* He caught it. He was smart and knew just the right time to strike.

Dickens proved he was a grrreat hunter. Then you know what he did? He brought it to me as a gift. I'm not woofing you. Gypsy rubbed against my side and then settled down next to me. She was nice, and so was Dickens. I trusted them.

What the woof was that dog talking about? My best friends were cats. And really, were we so very different? We had the same number of eyes, ears, legs, tails, noses, and mouths. We all had fur, and we liked to play, eat, and nap. The only difference I could think of is that we all had different purposes. But so what? If we all did the same thing, a lot would be left undone.

I decided right then and there if the other dogs didn't hang out with me just because I liked cats, then fine and dandy. I'm a dog that could think for myself. I didn't need them to think for me.

I ran to Dickens and yipped a "you're it" and hurried away with him closing in on my tail. As far as I'm concerned, cats are cool.

Let's just face it. We all are different. But that doesn't make any of us better than the other. Woof no! We all have a place and purpose on this earth. It doesn't matter if our color, our language, what makes up our families, what we eat, or how we celebrate holidays are different from the other. These things are what make life interesting, not scary.

Maybe if the other dogs had taken the time to know Gypsy and Dickens they would see that cats are nice. Maybe some cats have been bad to them because they were afraid of dogs. Maybe the cats had been told that dogs are dangerous by other cats.

I say that we should learn from each other and celebrate our differences. Why not learn each other's way of doing things? Who knows? If a cat thinks a mole is tasty, I might too, and if I didn't like mole, at least I've had a new experience with my cat-friend.

WINSTON WONDERS?

Do you have a friend that looks or acts differently from you? Do you have a friend that celebrates different holidays than you do? Have you been shy about talking to someone who is different from you? Why not give it a try?

❧ SCARED SILLY

Being Scared Doesn't Mean
You're a Chicken

High paw everyone! Winston Apple here, the TDIC (Top Dog in Charge) of Apple security, with my latest report: Being Scared.

I just had a woofin' good time with my buddy Soren. Dawg, I love that boy! When he comes to visit me and the folks, he lets me in and out and in and out and in and out allll I want. And he gives me yummy treats too. One of my favorites is shredded cheddar cheese. And I found out that when he feels guilty, I get a double portion.

Guilty you ask? Yeppers. Guilty.

Here's what happened. Soren was watching something called a football game on television with Sugar and Babe. I liked watching the game too because the peoples on the television threw a ball all the time. Sometimes they kicked it. But after a while the whole thing got pretty boring.

As the TDIC, I work really hard watching for sneaky squirrels and destructive deer, so since no one was really paying attention to me, I decided to take a nap in front of a floor heater. Ever seen one? It is a small box with wires that turn red and send out waves of warmth. Kinda like the sun. So, while everyone else watched whatever the woof football is, I circled my spot on the floor three times and plopped down in front of the floor heater to catch a few Z's.

Soon I was snoozing. I dreamed of chasing squirrels across fields of flowers and magically being able to run up trees after them. I love that dream. Anyway, just as I was closing in on a squirrel there was an explosion. Yep, you read me right. An explosion. Hands slapped together like thunder, everyone yelling—no they were screaming— "Yes! He caught it. Go, go, go!"

What the woof???

In my sleep-befuddled mind, I wondered, are we under attack? Had the house been bombed? Was the world ending? Even before I was fully awake, I sprang up on all fours and swung my head to the left and right, giving whoever or whatever the enemy was a good barking. I sounded the alarm, "Danger! Take cover under the table! Head for the hills."

Then, when I could focus, I saw Soren laughing. The folks were laughing too. Peoples, all I can say is they are lucky that there wasn't a puddle… or something worse… under me!

Well, after the ones who were supposed to love and care for me quit laughing, Soren gave me two handfuls of cheese. Heck, he can scare the fleas off of me any day for two handfuls of cheese. However, it did get sorta old the way they kept giggling at me every time they looked at me. Geeze, it wasn't that funny. I decided to ignore them, circle my spot on the floor three more times, and go back to sleep hoping for another squirrel dream, and just maybe this time I would sleep long enough to catch the silly thing.

Just because you get frightened, it doesn't mean you are a chicken or even a squirrel. It means you are cautious, and that can be a good thing. Also, when things take you by surprise, you have been given the instinct to flee to protect yourself. It's all good. So, if people laugh, let them. That just shows their brains are goofy like a squirrel. Arf!

WINSTON WONDERS?

What sort of things scare you? What do you do when you get scared? If someone is trying to scare you on purpose, be brave and ask them to stop. They have no business bullying you.

TELLING THE TRUTH

Even When You Don't Want To

High paw everyone! Winston Apple here, the TDIC (Top Dog in Charge) of Apple security, with my latest report: True Story.

Before I begin my report let me just say that there are some temptations that are bigger than I can resist, such as playing with forbidden balls. I mean, balls are my most, very, favoritist toys. Well, balls and stuffed hedgehogs, that is. So, it just isn't right to shove a ball in front of my nose for me to admire and then tell me I can't play with it. Not right at all! And that's just what my buddy Soren did to me the other day when he came over to play.

While my folks, Sugar and Babe, were busy working in the yard, Soren tossed a ball way up in the air and caught it with a huge catchy thing he wore on his left hand. He called it a glove.

I sat in the grass, trying to do my job as TDIC, but I couldn't resist watching that ball go up and down, up and down, got my heart to beating double-time. Peoples, I was ready to play. I jumped up and barked, "Throw it to me. Throw it to me."

Soren held the ball in front of me and said, "See this ball?"

Well, of course I see it. Woof, I can smell it. Now let's play.

"It is a special ball. It is signed by my most favorite baseball pitcher in the world."

Okay, who cares? Throw the ball.

"So, you can't play with it." Soren stuck the ball in the glove on his left hand and walked into the house.

Huh? What just happened here? Let's see. Soren is throwing a ball, shoves it in front of my face, and then says I can't play with it? Now that's just wrong. I couldn't have possibly heard him right.

Sugar called to me, "Winston? Time to go inside." Good. I needed to investigate this ball thing closer.

I found Soren in the family room watching cartoons. He had stuck his ball deep inside the glove on the couch and laid it next to him. I inched closer to it, stood on my hind legs and put my paws a respectable distance from it, and gave a little sniff.

"No Winston." Soren grabbed the ball and held it in his hands.

For woofing out loud. I was just giving it a little sniff. Geeze. I tried another tactic. I sat in front of him and gave him my most pitiful puppy-eye look. But no. He held on to that wonderful ball. Well, squirrels.

Good luck was on my side. Sugar called Soren to lunch. He put the ball back in the glove, looked at me, and placed them in the middle of the coffee table.

Ha! Did he actually think I couldn't get on

that table? Besides, I just wanted to see the ball. He'd never know I had given it a good sniffing. I may even lick it a couple of times.

I waited until I heard the dining room chairs scrape back. This meant they had all sat down to eat. Very carefully I jumped up on the table and slowly removed the ball from the glove with my teeth.

Oh, boy, did that ball feel good in my mouth. It was hard, but it had a soft skin that popped when I bit down. I couldn't help it. I bit it all over. Then I tossed it up and chased it when it hit the ground and rolled. What fun.

I played and played and played until I heard the chairs scrape. That meant they were finished eating. I rushed to pick up the ball because I needed to put it back in the glove.

That's when I saw the tooth marks allll over Soren's ball. Oh, boy, was I ever in trouble. I had to act fast. Soren's footsteps sounded down the hall. In a panic I rolled the ball behind the window drapes. Then I went to the other side of the room and pretended to be asleep.

When Soren reached for his ball and saw it

wasn't there, he said, "Wiiinnnston? Where is my ball?"

I tried to look innocent. Ears straight up, eyes bright, the tip of my tongue relaxed over my bottom teeth.

Ball? What ball?

Soren now stood over me. "Winston, did you get my ball?"

I tried to keep my ears up, but they betrayed me and melted down beside my face. I dropped my head and turned it away from him. My tail whapped a few times before I melted into a fuzzy black puddle, proving my guilt.

"Where is it, Winston?"

I kept my face turned away from him but cut eyes toward him. My tail whapped a few more times, then I looked up and gave him my best *I don't know* message.

Soren heaved a sigh and started looking around the room. My heart thudded faster and faster as he moved closer to the curtains.

Then he found it and yelled, "Winston. You bad boy!"

Busted.

He held the ball in my face. "Look at what you did."

I didn't do it, honest.

"I told you not to play with my ball. Now look at it."

What could I say? The evidence was all over the ball. I whined and crept toward him to lick an apology.

Just then, Babe walked into the room. "What's going on Soren?"

"Look what Winston did to my ball."

Babe looked at it and held it up. "Did you do this Winston?"

Yes! Yes, I did it! I'm sorry! I hung my head in shame.

Babe patted Soren on the shoulder. "I'll get you another ball signed, son."

What a relief. Babe came to my rescue.

Right then and there I vowed to never even look at the new ball.

Soren smiled and knelt down to scratch my head. "I forgive you boy. And I would have forgiven you even if I wasn't getting another ball."

He tossed the ball in the air and caught it. My

head went up and down as I watched. But I didn't budge from the spot where I sat. No sir. Not me.

"Hey Winston. Wanna play ball?"

Do I want to play ball? Does a frog jump? Of course I want to!

I ran around and around Soren while barking, *throw it to me! Throw it to me!*

We made such a racket that Babe came back into the room and said, "Hey, boys, maybe you need to take this game outside."

"Ok." Soren waved to me. "Come on, Winston! Let's go."

He didn't have to ask me twice. I ran to the door happy to be free from the guilt of my big lie and excited because I was going to play ball!

There are many times we might want to tell a lie. Maybe we say something that isn't true because we want to impress our friends. Sometimes it is a way to get out of something we don't want to do or to get something we want. For me, it was to keep from getting in trouble.

This may surprise you, but I've shaded the truth before, and you know what happens? I have to keep barking more lies to cover up my first one. I eventually get caught, and then I'm worse off than if I'd just barked the truth the first time.

Sugar and Babe make it safe for me to tell the

truth, but I do have to apologize. I may not get a treat that day, but that's okay because I promise myself that I'll do better next time. And believe me, if balls are involved, it will be difficult. But I can do it! Arf!

WINSTON WONDERS?

How does telling lies make you feel? Have you ever told a lie only to find it made the situation worse not better? Why do you think it is a good choice to always tell the truth?

MISTAKES...
THEY HAPPEN

Nobody's Pawfect

High paw everyone! Winston Apple here, the TDIC (Top Dog in Charge) of Apple security, with my latest report: Digging Myself into a Hole.

In case you didn't know, we Scotty dogs were born to dig. Digging is what we do when we hunt badgers or when we are bored or when we are trying to help our folks in the garden. Helping my folks in their garden was exactly my intention, only it didn't turn out so well. Here's what happened.

The day had started out so perfect. I sat in the yard keeping an eye out for sneaky squirrels while my folks, Babe and Sugar, raked all the winter leaves out of the flower beds. When the beds were all nice and clean, they got their shovels and dug holes. A *lot* of holes.

Hey, that looked like fun. After all, holes are my specialty. I could help them even without a shovel. When I trotted over to offer my help, though, they shooed me away. This kinda hurt my feelers. I mean, my paws are digging machines. Much better than those clumsy tools they used. Oh well, I went back to watching out for sneaky squirrels trying to steal seed from our bird feeders and destructive deer eating our bushes.

A while later the folks went inside and totally forgot about me. Or did they? Just maybe they realized I could do a much better job. I glanced at all the bedding plants that still sat on the porch waiting to be planted. That had to be it. I eased to the beds, looked at the door just to make sure I was right in my assumption, then glanced back at the beds, then back at the door. No sign of the folks returning. After a quick sniff I found the perfect spot to dig. I stretched my toes to limber them up and commenced.

At first, I gave the soil a few scratches. BowWowsers did that ever feel good to my paws. I dug faster, deeper, then even faster, and even deeper. Dirt was flying all over the place. In the trees, on the plants, on the driveway, on the front porch, on the sidewalk, and all over me, but I didn't care. I went deeper and deeper, who knew? I might even find a mole for the cat.

I was down to my ears in the hole when I heard the door slam. I looked up expecting a pat on the head and the folks thanking me for my good work. But noooo. Instead they yelled, "Winston! What on earth do you think you are doing? Get out of there."

Pardon me? I'm helping.

Sugar knelt down beside me and said, "Look at you, all covered with dirt." Then she picked me up. "And look at the mess you made."

I had to admit, it did look like a dirt bomb had exploded. I may have gotten a wee bit carried away. I licked her face with my most sincere "I'm sorry" apology.

"I forgive you." She put me down in the yard. "But you will have to have a bath."

A bath? Oh, no. Not a bath. I hate baths. My ears fell flat. I hung my head and stared up with my best contrite expression. But it didn't work. She just grabbed a broom and started sweeping while Babe finished planting. And then, you know what? He even used my hole to plant a small tree.

Later that evening after supper and after my bath, we sat on the clean porch and admired the flower beds.

Babe scratched behind my ears and said, "Thanks for your help, buddy."

I gave him a *you are welcome*-lick. Hey, I may have made a mistake by digging that big hole, but somehow it turned out all right anyway. Next time? They can forget me helping. Nothing is worth a bath. Arf!

We all make mistakes, don't we? We may break something when we are trying to help. We may call someone by the wrong name or give a wrong answer in school. The important thing is that we learn from our mistakes, so we won't make them again. I won't ever dig in the folks' flower beds again, that's for sure. Nope, I'll do my digging in the yard. Arf!

WINSTON WONDERS?

What kind of mistakes have you made? How did you handle it when you made a mistake? What did you learn from your mistake?

REFLECTION IN THE GLASS DOOR

Why Can't I Be Like Murray?

High paw everyone! Winston Apple here, the TDIC (Top Dog in Charge) of Apple security, with my latest report: Comparing Myself to Others.

Before I begin my report, you need to know that until a few days ago I used to love everything, including myself. I never gave a thought to what I looked like or what I could or couldn't do. But the other day something happened that made me aware that I was different.

What happened you wonder?

I saw my reflection in the glass door, and I didn't like it one little bit.

My best dog-friend, Murray, is a Goldendoodle, and he came over for the weekend. We always have fun running around the house and wrestling. But I'm still the TDIC, and there is always work to be done.

So, after a while of frolicking, it was time to do a security check, and I invited Murray to join me. I showed him my surveillance door, which is mostly glass, the perfect place to watch for sneaky squirrels that rob from the folks' bird feeders and destructive deer that eat their flowers and bushes.

While we sat looking out the door, I noticed in the reflection how much taller Murray was than me. Until that moment, I hadn't noticed. After all, when we wrestled, I usually pinned him down. I looked at Murray and noticed his legs were long. Me? I had short, stubby legs. Not only that, I liked his hair better than mine. It was a light reddish-gold color, and you could see his soulful brown eyes. I'm so black, and my eyes are so brown that I look like a blob with no eyes at all. Another thing. He had a nice, long nose, but mine looked like a box stuck on my face.

My list of complaints grew. His ears were soft and floppy. Mine are so pointed that you could stick hot dogs on them to roast over a fire. His tail was long and fluffy. Mine looks like a short spike.

Besides how he looked, there were more reasons I wished I was like Murray. For instance, since he was so tall, he could get anything he wanted off the kitchen counter. In fact, he told me how he stood on his hind legs and ate an entire pie.

Even when I stand on my hind legs, I can't reach above the second drawer. Murray could also get yummy snacks out of the trash anytime he wants. Not me. I have to wait until the folks, or my buddy Soren, give me any yummies.

After surveillance duty, Murray wanted to play, but I didn't feel like it. I just wanted to lay on my pillow and sulk. Heck, all those times I pinned him down? He probably just let me. It wasn't fair. Why wasn't I tall and strong? Why didn't I have golden hair so my eyes could be seen? Why was I a short, fuzzy, black blob with a big square nose?

For the rest of the day I laid on my bed with my boxy nose resting on my paws. I vowed to never, ever, never again look out that glass door. No. Not even a window. Why? Because I didn't like what I saw. In other words, I didn't like *me*.

I wanted to be like Murray.

Later that day, Soren came over for a visit. He was really excited about something. He waved a sheet of paper in his hand and said, "Winston, I got an A on the report I wrote about you."

Soren was reporting? Fine. He might as well since I'm not looking out my surveillance door anymore. I didn't move but did manage to gaze up at him with dark brown eyes he probably couldn't see, anyway.

"What's the matter boy?" He stroked my back. "Don'cha feel good?"

No, I feel awful. Horrible. But since he couldn't read my mind, I just gave him a teeny, tiny, lick.

"Listen to what I wrote about you."

Go ahead, buddy. Make me feel worse about myself, if that's possible.

He cleared his voice and started to read. "Scottish Terriers have strong, muscular, bodies.

Their eyes are bright and piercing. Their erect ears and tail show their keen alertness."

Did I hear him right? Muscular? Bright, piercing eyes? Erect ears and tail? Keen alertness? Well, come to think of it, this perfectly described my talent as the TDIC of Apple Security. I held my head up with interest and gave him my best, *well, go on* look.

"This breed are hunters."

Of course, I'm a hunter. I chase squirrels and deer, don't I?

"Scotties are bold, confident, and dignified. They are power in a small package."

This made me sit up straight and listen with my *alert* ears.

"Scotties have been a favorite breed for centuries. They have been the preferred breed of kings, queens, and presidents."

I held my head up. Kings? Queens? Presidents? Really? Right then and there I felt proud of who I was, after all, being the preferred dog of royalty and presidents, what's not to adore? And I was happy with how I was made. I promised myself to be the best me, ever.

All of a sudden, I felt like playing, so I ran to Murray and jumped on his back and barked, "Tag. You're it!" We had a great time. And when we got tired, we both stood guard at the glass door. This time the reflection showed a big, sweet dog, named Murray, and a small, bold, powerful dog, named Winston. Our reflections didn't change, but what did change was how I viewed it.

Hmmmm, I think I might change my name to Sir Winston. Sounds sort of regal. Whaddya think? Arf!

No matter who we are, there is no one just like us. We are all unique, in other words, different in a special way. So, instead of focusing on what we can't do we should focus on our specialness, what we can do. And then get better at it.

Murray's specialness is that he is a gentle giant that is family-friendly and is the best playmate ever! Goldendoodles are also perfect as service dogs. His breed only came into existence in the last few decades.

But *my* specialness is that I'm a hunter, a protector, and powerful. And my breed has been around for centuries. So why would I want to be any dog but me? From now on I'm going to be more powerful, keener, and the best protector ever. Arf!

WINSTON WONDERS?

What is special about you? What can you do well? What makes you uniquely you? What do you like about yourself?

WHAT THE WOOF?

Fishing for Flies

High paw everyone! Winston Apple here, the TDIC (Top Dog in Charge) of Apple security, with my latest report: A Little Misunderstanding.

It all started when my folks, Sugar and Babe, told me we were going fly fishing. Huh? I shook my head to clear my ears. Surely, I heard them wrong. But no, they packed all their fishing gear, and when my little buddy Soren came, we all crowded in the car and headed to our favorite stream to fish for flies. What the woof???

During the drive there I wondered about flies. In all the times I'd been to that stream, I didn't remember many there. While I was wondering, other thoughts drifted into my head. Like, where does one find a hook small enough to catch a fly?

Do you just keep flinging your fishing line in the air and hope one bites? And what if you catch a fly? How do you clean it? For that matter, how do you cook a fly? Roll it in cornmeal and fry it? Barbeque it on the grill? Stew it in a pot?

This just didn't make any sense. Besides, no matter how you cook flies, they taste awful—don't ask me how I know—and even if you liked the taste of the things, you'd have to have a bazillion of them to make a decent meal. Catching that many could take days, weeks, months—heck— even years!

Oh well, if this was what the folks and Soren wanted, who was I to complain. I decided it wasn't worth wondering about, so I nudged Soren's arm with my nose and laid my head on his lap for a good ear scratching.

After we arrived, I closely observed the preparation for catching flies. Soren grabbed his fishing pole out of the car. Have you ever seen a fishing pole? It had a round thing attached to it. He called this a reel. It had string wound around it and up the pole. On the end of this string he tied a little fuzzy thing that had a hook attached to it.

Right away I saw a problem. His hook was waaaaay too big for a fly. I ask you, how in the woof did he expect a fly to swallow that? And what fly would want to eat fuzzy things? They liked smelly stuff like garbage. I didn't bark this observation to him, though. I just kept my mouth shut and kept watching. Between you and me? This whole fly-fishing thing was getting more and more ridiculous.

Finally, Soren joined the folks, and they walked a little way into the stream where they threw their lines in the air, and yep, you guessed it. They didn't catch a single fly. Nope, their hooks went straight into the water. But they didn't quit. They rolled up their string and tried again… and again… and again.

All of a sudden, Soren let out a loud, "Whoop!" His pole bent nearly in half as he tried to wind up his string again. Only he wasn't upset that something had hold of his hook, he was really excited. He gave one mighty jerk and a flash of green, pink, and white glittered in the sunlight, then landed on the ground flopping all over the place.

What was that?

Soren took the hook out of its mouth and said, "It's a beauty, isn't it boy?" Then he held it up for me to investigate with my nose. "It's a trout fish."

First, I gave it a visual investigation. Long, thin, greenish gray on top with a stripe of pink below and white on the bottom. It had little specks all over the top. Its eyes were big and bulging, and there were slits behind the eyes. The slits moved up and down, up and down. Behind the slits were little flappers on either side. Soren told me the slits were gills, that was how fish breathed, and the flappers were fins helping them to swim.

Second, I gave it the sniff-and-lick procedure. It smelled clean with hints of moss and grass. Its skin was cold and soft on my tongue. Yeppers, while Soren didn't catch a fly, in my humble opinion he caught something much better. I

watched as he carried it back to the stream and gently held it in the water, rocking it back and forth a little before then letting it go. The fish glided away. It was a pretty sight.

Soon Soren was busy tying another fuzzy thing on the end of his string. I guessed he was going to try for a fly again. He held the fuzzy thing in front of me and said, "See this fly, Winston? I bet I'll catch an even bigger fish with it."

Wait? What?

It took a moment for the truth of this puzzlement to dawn on me. They weren't fishing for flies. They were fishing for fish using fuzzy things called flies. Well, why the woof didn't they just say that?

I found a nice grassy spot under a shade tree and flopped down to watch them fish for fish. As I watched them throw the fuzzy flies in the water, I felt thankful that we wouldn't be eating French fried flies for supper.

Sometimes we misunderstand what people mean, and we let that bother us. Like, if your friend says to you, "Stop being dumb," and you think your friend is calling you a bad name. But that isn't what your friend meant. Acting and being are two very different things, like flies and fish.

Maybe your teacher looks angry when she is listening to you tell her about a problem, but really, what she is doing is listening very closely and trying to think of how to help you. Her frown isn't anger, it is concern.

I thought I was having flies for supper, but as I watched and listened, I found out my mistake. So, give yourself some time to think things through, and if you are still confused, ask questions. Believe me, if I could talk, I'd been asking a lot of them. Arf!

WINSTON WONDERS?

Has anyone ever misunderstood something you said? Have you ever misunderstood something a friend said to you and your feelers were hurt? Have you ever thought someone didn't like you only to find out they were just having a really bad day?

ABOUT
THE TDIC

Winston Wallace Apple was born in the Windy Ridge Kennel in Leonard, TX, where Neal, aka, Babe, picked him out as a surprise for Linda, aka, Sugar. His stories began on a camping trip where, as a puppy, he saw his first turtle and was clearly perplexed. This inspired Linda to begin writing stories from his point of view, and she posted them on her Facebook page. Winston became so popular that she pitched an idea about an early reader book to the President and Creative Director at

Oghma Creative Media, Casey Cowan. Young Dragon Press Publisher Chrissy Willis worked closely with Linda and soon, *BOWWOW: Book of Winston's Words of Wisdom,* came into fruition.

Winston enjoys chasing destructive deer and sneaky squirrels. He loves tummy rubs and scratches behind his ears. He is currently barking new stories to Sugar because there is always something interesting the head of Apple Security needs to investigate.

LINDA APPLE (AKA SUGAR) is the author of seven books (nonfiction and fiction) as well as an inspirational/motivational speaker. She is published in sixteen of the Chicken Soup for the Soul books. Linda writes to inspire her readers of all ages. She has thirteen grandchildren, so it is easy to see why after being surprised with the gift of a cute Scottish Terrier puppy, her writing focused on inspiring children.

Her stories about Winston's experiences are based on actual occurrences, and she imagines what her perky pup might say about them if he had the chance. To her surprise when she posted these stories on her Facebook page, Winston was a big hit, and many asked for a Winston book. Thus, *BOWWOW: Book of Winston's Words of Wisdom,* was written.

Linda and Winston live in Northwest Arkansas with her husband Neal, aka Babe. She enjoys creating beauty through gardening and crafts and inspiring with her words, both written and spoken.

ABOUT THE ARTIST

DYLAN HALE HAS been creating works of art ever since he was four years old. His passion for all things artistic has led him down some interesting paths in his career, including cake decorator, muralist, designing advisor, teacher, and most recently, an illustrator with Oghma Creative Media.

A native of Bentonville, Arkansas, Dylan is a cake decorator by trade. At fifteen, he began decorating desserts for friends and family and went on to work for some of the most well-known bakeries in Northwest Arkansas, as well as placing bronze in the 2018 Oklahoma State Sugar Art Show (known by some as the "Olympics of Cake Decorating").

While his enthusiasm for creating cakes is always present, his heart lies in the classroom with his students. Graduating with his BFA in Art Education from the University of Arkansas at Fayetteville, Dylan jumped headfirst into the teaching world. In Bentonville, he currently teaches graphic design to high schoolers and general art to 5th graders. While he prefers to be called "Mr. Hale" or "Mr. H," being split between two schools students sometimes forget his name and simply call him "Mr. Moustache."

As an artist, Dylan's work contains a wide range of styles and techniques, from intriguing drawings to twisted sculptures. Although he is comfortable with any media, his favorites are pen & ink, watercolors, and printmaking when he can.

Want to know more about Winston?

Check out his website at
http://winstonswisdom.com

You can even send him an e-mail!
(No pee mails accepted)

Look for more books coming from Winston and his friends in 2021!

🐾 A Christmas Tail (Winston Learns About Christmas)

by Linda C. Apple & Winston

🐾 Critter Invasion

by Clarissa Willis

🐾 Twas the Night Before Gus Meets his Fur-Ever Family

by Sherry Roberts

🐾 The Lantaka

by Jonathan Bouw

🐾 Fred Finds his Fur-Ever Home

by Ruth Weeks

🐾 Where did Frank Go?

by Seth Stewart